Cassie the Concert Fairy

To Orren and Myah with love

Special thanks to Rachel Elliot

ISBN 978-0-545-48482-4

Previously published as *Pop Star Fairies #7: Una the Concert Fairy* by Orchard U.K. in 2012.

12 11 10 9 8 7 6 5 4 3 2 1 13 14 15 16 17 18/0

Printed in the U.S.A. 40

This edition first printing, March 2013

Cassie the Concert Fairy

by Daisy Meadows

SCHOLASTIC INC.

Fairyland Music Festival
A-OK trailer
Rehearsal tent
Star Village
Picnic hill
Beach

Jack Frost's Ice Castle
Campsite
Girls' tent
Main Stage
Karaoke tent
The Harbor
Café
Rainspell Island

It's about time for the world to see
The legend I was born to be.
The prince of pop, a dazzling star,
My fans will flock from near and far.

But superstar fame is hard to get
Unless I help myself, I bet.
I need a plan, a cunning trick
To make my stage act super-slick.

Seven magic clefs I'll steal —
They'll give me true superstar appeal.
I'll sing and dance, I'll dazzle and shine,
And superstar glory will be mine!

Contents

Trouble on Rainspell Island

"My autograph book is almost full," said Kirsty Tate, turning the blue pages happily. "We've met so many famous stars at the festival!"

"Mine, too," said Rachel Walker, who had her pink autograph book open on her lap. "I can't believe it's our last day already."

"The Rainspell Island Music Festival has been so much fun, I can hardly imagine going back to ordinary life," said Kirsty with a laugh. "I wish it didn't have to end."

Kirsty and Rachel were sitting on stools outside their tent. They had really enjoyed being special guests of their favorite music group, The Angels. The afternoon sun seemed to light up the tents around them with a golden glow.

"It looks like it's enchanted, doesn't it?"

said Rachel. "Almost as magical as the fairy campsite we visited with Jessie the Lyrics Fairy."

Kirsty and Rachel were good friends with many fairies, and they had often visited Fairyland and ruined Jack Frost's evil schemes. On the first day of the festival, they had stumbled across one of his most mischievous plans yet. Jack Frost had stolen seven magic music clef necklaces from the Superstar Fairies. He planned to use them to become a superstar himself.

He had given most of the clefs to his goblins, who brought them to the Rainspell Island Music Festival. There, Kirsty and Rachel had tracked them down one by one. Jack Frost had disguised himself as rapper Jax Tempo to impress people at the festival, but he didn't fool the girls for long.

The Superstar Fairies needed their clefs to look after superstars everywhere, and Kirsty and Rachel were determined to help their friends. So far, they had helped six fairies get their magic clefs back, but Jack Frost still had one. It belonged to Cassie the Concert Fairy.

"I just hope we can find the last clef before the end of the festival," said Kirsty. "Maybe we should go and look for Cassie."

"But Queen Titania always says that we should wait for the magic to come to us," Rachel reminded her, turning another page of her autograph book. "Just look at all the amazing people we've met this week, Kirsty. Dakota May, Jacob Bright, A-OK, Sasha Sharp, The Groove Gang . . . and weren't all the concerts wonderful?"

"Yes, and tonight's concert will be the best yet," said Kirsty. "There's even going to be a surprise superstar there. I hope we can stop Jack Frost from ruining it."

Just then, The Angels came walking around the side of the tent. They were wearing long floral dresses, and had flowers woven into their hair.

"Hi, girls," said Lexy. "We're on our way to watch the main stage being set up for tonight's concert. Would you like to come along?"

Rachel and Kirsty both smiled.

"Definitely!" they said together.

"Let's go!" said Emilia with a grin.

The girls and The Angels made their way out of the campsite and through the festival.

"The main stage is always super busy," said Serena as they strolled past the exciting activity tents in Star Village. "I love the hustle and bustle of people setting up the sound systems and the stars rehearsing."

It sounded wonderful! They passed the Food Fest picnic area and walked around a large tree.

"Here we are!" said Lexy.

But they were in for a big surprise. The stage was empty! No one was setting up for the concert, and no one was rehearsing. A few workers were standing around at the sides of the stage, looking very gloomy. Melody Jones, the festival organizer, walked across the stage toward the girls, her face serious.

"Melody, what's wrong?" asked Emilia, leading the others up onto the stage.

"I'm afraid the electricity isn't working," Melody replied.

"That means no lights, no sound, and no concert!"

At that moment, there was a strange cracking noise from backstage. Then they heard a loud *bang*, and a fountain of water sprayed onto the stage!

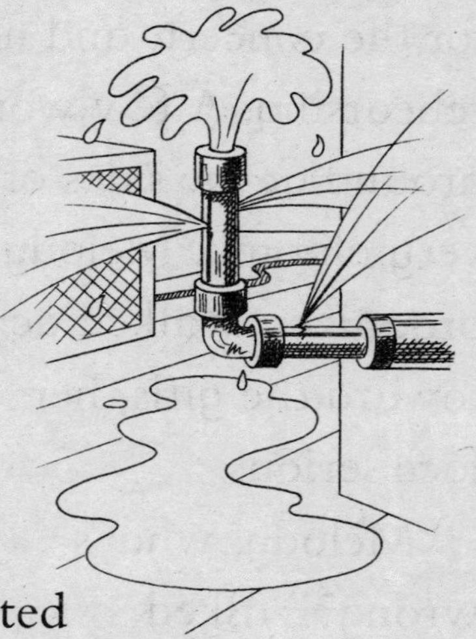

Rachel, Kirsty, and The Angels darted backward. Melody screamed as a wave of water rolled toward them.

"A pipe must have burst!" Serena exclaimed. "We have to get off the stage!"

They all hurried down to the front row of the stands.

"That was close!" said Emilia.

"What are we going to do?" Melody cried.

She was panicking, but The Angels stayed calm.

"We'll have to move the concert to another area of the festival," said Lexy. "Melody, is there somewhere else we can use?"

Before Melody could reply, her cell phone rang. She answered it and her face fell.

"Looks like bad news again," Rachel whispered.

"What happened now?" asked Serena when Melody hung up the phone.

"Our special guest for tonight's finale has a sore throat and can't sing!" said Melody in dismay.

Just then, Rachel noticed something near the side of the stage. One of the spotlights seemed to be giving out a tiny pool of light. She gently touched Kirsty's arm.

"Look over there," she whispered. "How can the spotlight be working if there's no electricity?"

"It must be magic," said Kirsty in excitement. "Come on, let's investigate."

Melody and The Angels were busy discussing how to save the festival finale, so they didn't notice the girls heading over to the spotlight. As Rachel and Kirsty moved closer, the little light darted away from them and into the stands on the side. The girls weaved in and out of the stands until they were out of sight of the others. Once they stopped, the beam of light seemed to grow. Then it vanished in a puff of fairy dust! A tiny fairy was fluttering in front of them. She was wearing a pretty orange dress with glittery purple tights.

"It's Cassie the Concert Fairy!" said Kirsty. "Hello!"

"Hi, girls!" said Cassie, flashing them a big smile. She had a light sprinkling of freckles across her cheeks and nose, and her strawberry blond hair was twisted into a thick braid.

"We were hoping you'd find us," said Rachel. "It's the last day of the festival."

"I know," said Cassie. "I have to get my magic clef back before tonight's concert. Without it, the finale of the Rainspell Island Music Festival will be ruined!"

"Things are already going wrong," said Rachel. "There's no electricity here, and a pipe just burst backstage."

"Oh, no," said Cassie, looking upset. "Girls, will you help me look for the clef?"

"Of course we will," Kirsty promised. "Let's go and find out what Melody is going to do."

Cassie flitted into the pocket of Rachel's jean jacket, and the girls returned to the front row of the stands.

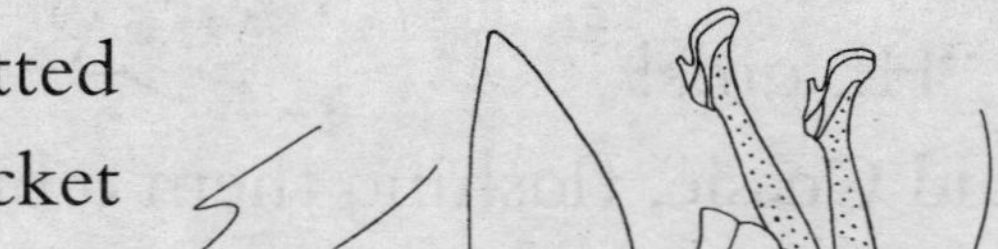

"I guess you're right," Lexy was saying to Melody, looking very disappointed. "It's just such a shame for the festival to end like this, after such a great week."

"What do you mean?" asked Rachel.

Melody and The Angels turned to look at the girls.

"We're going to have to cancel the final concert," Serena explained. "With no electricity and no special guest, everyone is just going to have to go home early."

Suddenly, they heard the squeal of an electric guitar. A haze of dry ice rose from the stage floor. Then the stage lights went on, and they saw a spiky-haired figure in a glittering blue jacket, striking a pose on top of a speaker.

"The electricity's back on!" cried Melody in relief.

“It’s Jack Frost!” Kirsty whispered to Rachel.

He was dressed in his Jax Tempo disguise. As the girls watched, he leaped off the speaker. Behind him, his band strutted onto the stage. They were wearing glittering green outfits and their enormous shiny green shoes were glistening under the spotlights.

“Goblins!” said Rachel. “What is Jack Frost up to now?”

Jax Tempo bounded across the stage, performing the rap that Kirsty and Rachel had heard before.

"I'm no fool
It's the number one rule,
I'm supercool!"

His dancing was wonderful, and his sense of rhythm was perfect. Behind him, his goblin band threw themselves into fast, complicated break-dancing moves.

“I know that he’s up to no good,” Kirsty whispered, “but he’s putting on a pretty great show.”

Rachel nodded and glanced over at The Angels. They were dancing along to the music.

“He’s fantastic!” Lexy said.

Jack Frost jumped back onto the speaker and thrashed out a long final riff on his guitar. He ended his rap perfectly! As the final note rang out, everyone who was watching burst into applause.

"Wonderful!" Melody exclaimed. "Jax, I want you to star in our festival finale — your performance was incredible!"

"I'll be there!" said Jack Frost with a wicked grin. He leaped up again and then slid along the floor on his knees, strumming his electric guitar in triumph.

Kirsty noticed a necklace swinging around on top of the guitar strap on Jack Frost's chest. It was a music clef!

"Rachel, Jack Frost has Cassie's magic clef around his neck!" she whispered.

"Jack Frost might be a great performer, but it's only because he stole Cassie's magic clef," said Rachel. "It's not fair to the other bands!"

"We have to get it back," said Kirsty in a determined voice.

"Girls, we're going to the festival office

to finalize the concert arrangements," said Emilia. "We'll see you later, OK?"

"OK," Rachel and Kirsty replied with a wave.

They waited until Melody and The Angels had gone, and then they walked up onto the stage. Jack Frost had his back to them. Kirsty folded her arms across her chest, and Rachel put her hands on her hips.

"Jax!" said Rachel.

Jack Frost whirled around. When he saw the girls, he scowled.

"Not you two again!" he said. "Go away — now!"

"Don't forget, we know who you really are," said Kirsty.

"*And* we know how you're putting on such a great performance," Rachel added. "That clef doesn't belong to you, so give it back to Cassie."

"No way!" Jack Frost snarled. "This is my big break, and you can't stop me. The world deserves to know about Jax Tempo!"

Before the girls could reply, he sent bolt after bolt of icy magic flying toward them. Kirsty and

Rachel dove aside as Jack Frost jumped off the stage and sprinted away. The goblins followed him as fast as they could, pushing and shoving one another, and cackling with laughter.

"He told you!" giggled a freckled goblin as he barged past Rachel.

"Go away, pesky humans!" yelled another.

"Let's follow them!" Rachel cried, running down the stage steps. "Come on, Kirsty, we can't let them get away!"

The girls chased after the racing goblins and their bad-tempered boss.

"They're heading out onto the festival grounds!" Kirsty panted. "Faster, Rachel, we're going to lose them!"

They saw a glittery green leg disappearing around the corner of a hot-dog stand. But when they raced around the stand, both Jack Frost and the goblins had vanished. Cassie popped her head out of Rachel's jacket pocket.

"Find somewhere out of sight to hide," she said. "We'll find them much more quickly if you girls are fairies, too."

They ducked behind a souvenir booth and Cassie fluttered out of Rachel's pocket. She raised her wand and flew around Rachel and Kirsty, scattering rainbow-colored fairy dust. It tickled as it softly landed on them and lifted them into the air, surrounding them in a whirl of color. They shrank to fairy-size, and beautiful, delicate wings appeared on their shoulders.

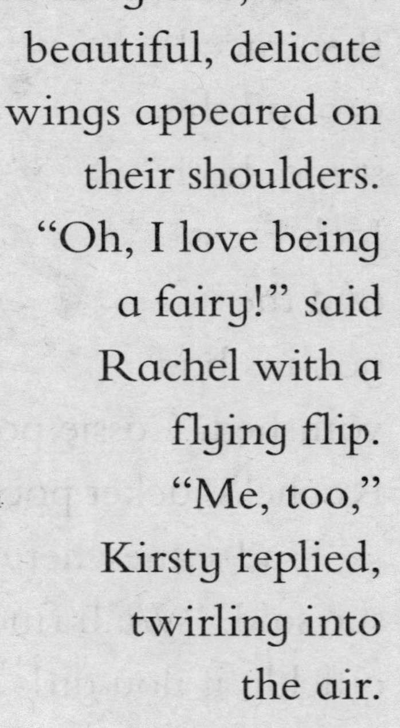

"Oh, I love being a fairy!" said Rachel with a flying flip.

"Me, too," Kirsty replied, twirling into the air.

"I'm glad," said Cassie with a laugh. "Come on, let's find Jack Frost and stop him from causing any more trouble!"

The three friends swooped high into the sky and looked down at the bustling crowds of the festival. It was a wonderful sight.

"There's so much going on down there," said Rachel. "Look at all the colors!"

"Yes," said Kirsty. "Lots of reds and yellows and greens. How are we going to spot the goblins among all those people?"

"Look over there," said Cassie, pointing to the Food Fest area. "Why is that crowd gathering? Maybe the goblins are putting on another performance!"

"Let's find out," said Rachel.

They zoomed down and hid among the leaves of a tree close to the crowd. The people were standing around a large picnic blanket, where A-OK, Sasha Sharp, The Groove Gang, Dakota May, and Jacob Bright were all having a picnic together.

"Some of the biggest superstars from the festival are here," said Kirsty. "No wonder they've attracted such a crowd. Ooh, this gives me a great idea for the finale concert!"

"But first we have to find Cassie's magic clef necklace," said Rachel.

The picnic looked like a lot of fun. The superstars were singing and jamming together. It was almost like a mini concert! The girls were enjoying listening to the music, but then Rachel gasped.

"Look — at the edge of the crowd!"

She pointed at a flash of ice blue darting through the crowd, followed by several flashes of green.

"It's Jack Frost and the goblins!" cried Cassie.

"I have an idea," Rachel said. "Cassie, can you use your magic to make your voice sound like it's in the crowd? Jack Frost will stop if he thinks there are fans around him!"

"Let's try it," said Kirsty.

Cassie tapped her wand against her throat and chanted a spell.

"To stop the mischief Jack began,
Make me sound just like a fan!"

A ribbon of fairy dust wound from the tip of her wand and circled her neck. When she spoke again, her voice sounded as if it came from out in the crowd.

"Look, there's Jax Tempo!" she shouted. "He's in the ice-blue jacket! I heard that he's the surprise star at tonight's finale! Let's get his autograph!"

The people who were standing around the stars' picnic turned to Jack Frost, who stopped in his tracks. He grinned and waved at them all.

"Hello, fans!" he said with a giggle. "I know I'm fabulous. Try not to faint with excitement!"

The goblins elbowed people out of the

way, clearing a path for Jack Frost like bodyguards.

"Stand clear. Get out of the star's personal space!" they shouted. "Make way! Make way! The famous Jax Tempo is coming through!"

"Let's follow them!" said Kirsty.

The three fairies flew out from the leaves and hid behind a fluttering flag, close to where Jack Frost and his goblins were showing off.

"We just have to swoop down and get the magic clef while he's distracted," said Rachel.

"That's easier said than done," Cassie said, sounding worried. "There are hundreds of people milling around — we'd be spotted if we flew down there now."

"We'll just have to wait until he's alone," said Kirsty.

Jack Frost was making his way toward his trailer. He gave a final smile and wave, then disappeared into the trailer with his goblins. As the door slammed, the three fairies exchanged looks of despair.

“How are we going to get the magic clef now?” groaned Cassie. “Even if we could get into the trailer without being seen, it’s *full* of goblins!”

“I’m not going to lose to Jack Frost!” said Kirsty in a determined voice. “Listen, I think I have an idea. He loves being famous, right?”

“Right,” agreed Cassie and Rachel.

“I bet that he’d love to be on TV,” Kirsty continued. “How about we disguise ourselves as goblins and pretend that we want to film him for a Goblin TV show? He might let us into the trailer, and then at least we’ll have a chance to get the clef back.”

Cassie looked doubtful.

"That could be really dangerous," she said. "What if he sees through the disguise? We could be trapped in the trailer with him."

"I think it's worth the risk," said Rachel bravely. "If we don't get that clef back, Jax Tempo will be the only act on the stage tonight. We're not going to let that happen!"

"Thank you!" said Cassie. "I'm so grateful to have you both on my team."

The three friends flew down to the trailer and hid in the long grass behind it.

They made sure that no one was watching, and then Cassie waved her wand. Instantly, Kirsty and Rachel changed to goblin-size. They looked at each other and giggled. Their skin was green, and their ears were long and pointy.

Kirsty had a microphone in her hand and was disguised as a Goblin TV reporter. Rachel was carrying a goblin-size camera on her right shoulder. Each of them was wearing a hat with GOBLIN TV on it.

"You look terrible!" said Rachel with a squawking goblin laugh.

"You, too!" Kirsty chuckled.

Cassie tucked herself under Kirsty's hat, and then the girls walked around to the front of the trailer and knocked on the door. It was opened by one of Jack Frost's backup dancers.

"What do you want?" he snapped at them.

"Hi, we're here from Goblin TV," said Rachel. "We want an exclusive interview with Jack Frost. It will be aired on every single goblin channel, and everyone will know about the famous Jax Tempo!"

The goblin's mouth fell open, and there was a sudden excited chatter from the goblins inside the trailer.

"Let them in — right now!" roared Jack Frost's voice.

The goblin at the door stepped aside, and Kirsty and Rachel walked into the trailer. It was dark inside, and it smelled of bad breath and old socks. When their eyes adjusted to the light, the girls saw Jack Frost lying back on a fancy blue chair. The goblins were standing around him and popping grapes into his mouth.

"Camera rolling," said Rachel, zooming in on Jack Frost's face.

"So what's it like living the life of a famous superstar?" asked Kirsty, sticking her microphone under Jack Frost's nose.

"Fantastic — the silly humans adore me!" said Jack Frost with a sneer. "I've got what it takes to make it all the way to the top, and no one's going to stop me!"

"And could you explain for the viewers how you cleverly stole the magic clefs from the Superstar Fairies?" asked Kirsty.

"It was a work of genius!" Jack Frost boasted. "I snuck into their dressing room while the fairies were trying on their silly outfits. Ha, ha!"

Rachel and Kirsty could only manage weak giggles at this.

"Um, could I get a close-up of the magic clef you're wearing, for the viewers?" asked Rachel, hoping that he would take the necklace off for her.

"No problem," said Jack Frost.

He held out the clef on its chain, without taking it off. Rachel glanced at Kirsty as she filmed the clef. What were they going to do now?

"So, Jack, what would you say to your critics?" asked Kirsty, thinking fast.

"Critics?" he snarled, sitting up very straight. "What critics?"

The goblins backed away and huddled in a corner of the trailer.

"Well, some goblins are saying that you're only a superstar because of the magic clef," Kirsty explained, shrugging her shoulders. "They say that without it you'd be a horrible singer."

The goblins in the corner gave scared gasps, and Kirsty held her breath. It was very dangerous to make Jack Frost angry.

"That's not true!" he bellowed, pulling the necklace off and scowling at Kirsty. "I don't need magic to be amazing — I have the Frost Factor, and I'm going to prove it!"

"What do you mean?" Rachel asked.

"Hold this," said Jack Frost, thrusting the necklace into Kirsty's hand. "I'll sing my song without the magic clef, and you'll see that I don't need those pesky fairies to be a star!"

He jumped up and started to sing:

"I'm no fool

It's the number one rule,

I'm supercool!"

Rachel clapped her hands over her ears. His rapping sounded like nails being dragged down a chalkboard. Kirsty saw Jack Frost's eyes widen — he knew how bad he sounded.

"Now, Cassie!" she cried.

Cassie fluttered out from under Rachel's hat and put her hands on the magic clef. As soon as she touched it, it shrank to fairy-size. Jack Frost stopped rapping and gave a howl of rage.

"What are you doing?" he yelled. "Traitors! Since when have goblins helped fairies? Are you crazy? I'll turn you into toadstools for this!"

"They're not goblins," said Cassie, glaring at him. "They're two very brave human beings!"

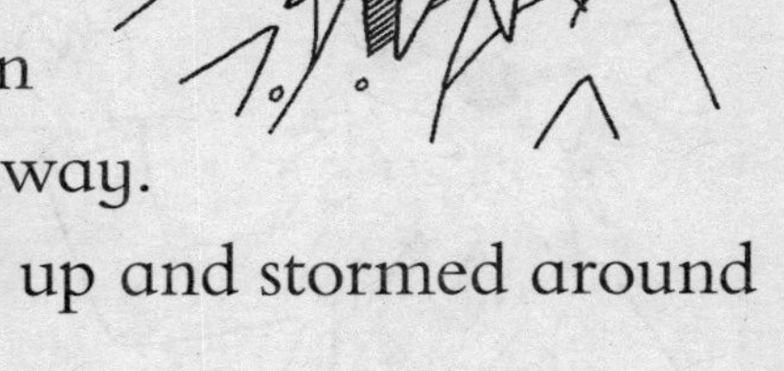

With a wave of her wand, Rachel's and Kirsty's goblin disguises melted away. Jack Frost jumped up and stormed around the trailer.

"You interfering humans!" he screeched. "You nosy little fairy! I never wanted to perform in your concert finale, anyway. I'll have my revenge on you all for this!"

"It's your own fault," said Rachel. "You stole the Superstar Fairies' clefs, and that was wrong."

"You can't tell me what to do!" Jack Frost shouted. "I've had enough of the Rainspell Island Music Festival. We're going back to the Ice Castle — *right now*! Goblins, you're coming with me!"

Jack Frost stood in the center of the trailer and snapped his fingers, expecting the goblins to scurry to his side. But none of them moved.

"Now!" he bellowed. "We don't need awful music festivals and silly pop songs."

"But I've been having fun," whined one of the goblins. "I don't want to leave!"

"I like it here," complained another goblin. "Why do we have to go?"

"WHAT?" hollered Jack Frost. "I'll make you sorry for disobeying me! I'll make you wish you'd never heard of pop music!"

"Let's get out of here!" said Cassie to the girls, fluttering toward the door.

While Jack Frost was shouting, Kirsty, Rachel, and Cassie slipped away. They could still hear his yells when they reached the main concert stage.

"We have to tell The Angels that they've lost their star performer," said Rachel. "Jax Tempo has disappeared — hopefully forever! I feel sorry for The Angels, though. They've been working so hard to make this concert a success."

"I have an idea about that," said Kirsty with a grin. Melody and The Angels were on the stage, managing the workers who were testing the sound system.

"Hi, girls!" said Serena, smiling at them.

"Hi, Serena," said Kirsty. "We've got good news and bad news. . . ."

At first, Melody and The Angels were worried when they heard that Jax Tempo had gone home. But when Kirsty explained her idea, their faces brightened.

"I thought of it when I saw all the superstars having a picnic together," she said. "How about putting all the acts onstage together?"

"That could work!" said Melody.

"I think it's a great idea," said Emilia. "There's been nothing like that at the festival before — it'll be amazing!"

"I'd better start organizing it then," said Melody with a smile. "Thanks, Kirsty!"

The girls went back to Cassie, who was waiting for them in the empty stands. Her eyes were sparkling with excitement.

"Girls, you've done so much to help me and the other Superstar Fairies," she said. "Now that I have my magic clef back, the Fairyland Music Festival can go ahead. Would you like to come as our guests of honor?"

"Yes, please!" said Rachel and Kirsty.

They both loved going to Fairyland, and it was even more exciting now that all seven clefs were safe. They knew that time would stand still in the human world while they were visiting the fairies, so no one would miss them while they were away.

Cassie waved her wand, and a glittering bubble surrounded the girls. It lifted them into the air, gently spinning. Then it popped in a puff of fairy dust, and Rachel and Kirsty found themselves in the royal box at the Fairyland Music Festival!

"Welcome, Rachel!" said a musical voice beside the girls. "Welcome, Kirsty!"

The girls turned and saw that they were sitting next to Queen Titania and King Oberon.

"Once again, you have proved yourselves loyal friends of Fairyland," said King Oberon. "This is going to be a wonderful festival, thanks to you."

"It's starting!" said the queen.

The stage looked magnificent, with lights of every color and garlands of flowers looped around the equipment. The stands were filled with excited fairies, whose gauzy wings glimmered in the sunlight. Spotlights swept across the crowd, and cheers rose up as a very stylish-looking fairy appeared on the stage.

"It's Destiny the Rock Star Fairy!" said Rachel.

"Welcome to the Fairyland Music Festival!" Destiny announced. "It's great

to see you all here — especially our guests of honor, Rachel and Kirsty. Without them, there wouldn't even be a festival!"

The crowd cheered again, and Rachel and Kirsty smiled and waved. They could see lots of their fairy friends watching from the stands.

"So," Destiny went on, "without any further ado, put your hands together for . . . the Music Fairies!"

It was a wonderful concert. The Music Fairies and the Dance Fairies all performed, along with many other unforgettable acts. Kirsty and Rachel clapped until their hands were sore!

Halfway through the concert, Rachel nudged Kirsty.

"Look over there," she said with a surprised smile.

At the back of the audience, they could see Jack Frost and his goblins. They were still wearing their festival outfits. Jack Frost was scowling and his arms were folded across his chest, but one of his big feet was tapping in time to the music.

The concert was a huge success. Best of all was the grand finale, when all the Superstar Fairies performed together with Destiny.

The show ended with fireworks exploding from the front of the stage, and then the Superstar Fairies fluttered up to the

royal box and hovered in front of the girls.

"Thank you both so much," said Cassie. "We couldn't have done any of this without you."

"It was our pleasure!" said Rachel.

They hugged each of the Superstar Fairies, and then Queen Titania stood up to speak.

"It has been wonderful to have you here as our guests," she said. "But now it is time to send you back to Rainspell Island. You have another festival finale to enjoy."

She waved her wand, and the stands and fairies around them seemed to melt away. Rachel and Kirsty were caught up in a golden whirlpool. When it finally disappeared, they were back on Rainspell Island.

That evening at the final concert of the Rainspell Island Music Festival, Rachel and Kirsty were standing in the front row with Rachel's parents, cheering and dancing along to the music. The stage was full of famous superstars for the last performance of the concert.

"Rachel! Kirsty!" called Melody, dashing toward them from the side of the stage. "How would you like to go up onstage with all of the stars for the finale?"

The girls nodded eagerly, and a few seconds later they were standing in a line between Dakota May and Jacob Bright. Everyone had their arms around one another's shoulders. The atmosphere was electric! The moon shone down on them as they sang a final song.

"It's like magic!
Let's work together to get the job done.
It's like magic!
If we help one another,
we'll have lots of fun."

As the last notes of the song rang out and the audience burst into deafening applause, Rachel looked across the sea of faces. She saw her parents beaming with pride in the front row, and waved to them.

As the applause died away, The Angels stepped forward.

"We would like to offer a very special thank-you to two important people," said Lexy.

"Just a few hours ago, it was looking as if this final concert would have to be canceled," Emilia added.

"But thanks to Rachel and Kirsty, this finale has been the best I've ever seen!" finished Serena. "Take a bow, Rachel Walker and Kirsty Tate!"

Feeling shy but very proud, the girls stepped forward and bowed to the

audience. The superstars gathered around them and burst into a final encore, and Rachel and Kirsty exchanged happy smiles as the audience cheered.

"A fairy festival and a concert all in one night," said Kirsty, squeezing her best friend's hand. "Isn't this amazing?!"

"We are so lucky," Rachel agreed. "Oh, Kirsty, I don't think summer vacations get any better than this!"

THE FASHION FAIRIES

Kirsty and Rachel helped find all
of the magic music clefs for
the Superstar Fairies.

Now they need to help the Fashion Fairies!
Read on for a special sneak peek of

Miranda
the Beauty Fairy!

A Splash of Magic

"This is amazing, Rachel!" Kirsty exclaimed. Her eyes wide, she stared up at the enormous glittering steel and glass building in front of them. Across the entrance was TIPPINGTON FOUNTAINS SHOPPING CENTER in blue lights.

"Yes, isn't it?" Rachel agreed. "I'm so glad you're staying with me for the break so you're here for the grand opening, Kirsty."

"Me, too," Kirsty said eagerly. "And I'm really looking forward to seeing Jessica Jarvis!" The famous supermodel Jessica Jarvis was the special guest at the new shopping mall's opening ceremony. A crowd of people had already gathered, waiting for the ceremony to begin.

"I think we're just in time for the parade," Mrs. Walker said, locking her car. "Come along, girls."

Rachel, Kirsty, and Mrs. Walker hurried to join the crowd. Moments later, the first float appeared around the side of the building.

"Every shop in the mall has its own

float, Kirsty," Rachel explained. "Look, the first one is Tippington Toys."

The float rumbled slowly toward them. A huge inflatable teddy bear sat on the back of the truck. Also on the float were girls dressed as rag dolls with ruffled dresses and pigtails made of yellow yarn, as well as a boy wearing a red soldier uniform. They waved to the crowd as they passed by.

"The next one is The Book Nook," Kirsty said, reading the painted banner draped across the float.

The Book Nook float carried people dressed as characters from storybooks. The girls saw Snow White, Cinderella, and Pinocchio. The Sweet Scoop Ice-Cream Parlor float came next, with its giant foam ice-cream cones and ice pops.

"That ice cream looks yummy!" Kirsty laughed.

Rachel sniffed the air. "I can smell something yummy, too," she said. . . .

SPECIAL EDITION

Three Books in Each One– More Rainbow Magic Fun!

Joy the Summer Vacation Fairy
Holly the Christmas Fairy
Kylie the Carnival Fairy
Stella the Star Fairy
Shannon the Ocean Fairy
Trixie the Halloween Fairy
Gabriella the Snow Kingdom Fairy
Juliet the Valentine Fairy
Mia the Bridesmaid Fairy
Flora the Dress-Up Fairy
Paige the Christmas Play Fairy
Emma the Easter Fairy
Cara the Camp Fairy
Destiny the Rock Star Fairy
Belle the Birthday Fairy
Olympia the Games Fairy
Selena the Sleepover Fairy
Cheryl the Christmas Tree Fairy
Florence the Friendship Fairy
Lindsay the Luck Fairy